Karen's Cowboy

Other books by
Ann M. Martin

Snail Mail No More
P. S. Longer Letter Later
(written with Paula Danziger)
Leo the Magnificat
Rachel Parker, Kindergarten Show-off
Eleven Kids, One Summer
Ma and Pa Dracula
Yours Turly, Shirley
Ten Kids, No Pets
With You and Without You
Me and Katie (the Pest)
Stage Fright
Inside Out
Bummer Summer

For older readers:

Missing Since Monday
Just a Summer Romance
Slam Book

THE BABY-SITTERS CLUB series
THE BABY-SITTERS CLUB mysteries
THE KIDS IN MS. COLMAN'S CLASS series
BABY-SITTERS LITTLE SISTER series
(see inside book covers for a complete listing)

BABY-SITTERS
Little Sister

Karen's Cowboy
Ann M. Martin

Illustrations by Susan Crocca Tang

A
LITTLE APPLE
PAPERBACK

SCHOLASTIC INC.
New York Toronto London Auckland Sydney
Mexico City New Delhi Hong Kong

The author gratefully acknowledges
Gabrielle Charbonnet
for her help
with this book.

Karen's Cowboy

How Scary Is Too Scary?

"Aaah!" cried Andrew. He grabbed my arm and squeezed it hard. I winced, but I did not tell him to stop. We were watching a Halloween show on TV. It was called *The Scaredy-Cat Ghost*. It was about a ghost who was so scared of everything that he forgot he was supposed to be scary himself. Parts of the show were funny, but some parts were spooky. Every time there was a spooky part, Andrew shrieked and grabbed my arm. I would probably have bruises the next day.

Now you know about the TV program, but you do not know anything about me, or Andrew, or why we were watching TV on a school night. Well, I am Karen Brewer. I am seven years old, and I live in Stoneybrook, Connecticut. I have blonde hair and blue eyes. Andrew is my little brother. He is four going on five, which is why he was the one grabbing my arm and I was the one being grabbed. We were watching TV on a Tuesday night because it was a special Halloween show, and Halloween was only three weeks away! We were already getting into the spirit. Spirit . . . ghost . . . get it? I made a Halloween joke.

"Aaah!" cried Andrew. His fingers clutched my arm again. I winced again. With his other hand, Andrew grabbed a sofa cushion and held it in front of his face. He peeped over the top of it. On the TV screen, the Scaredy-Cat Ghost was floating down a hallway in a haunted house. The Scaredy-Cat Ghost looked terrified. So did Andrew. I just felt excited, as if I were in a roller coaster car at the top of a hill, about to go down. I love being a little tiny bit scared.

When the Scaredy-Cat Ghost saw a shadow cross the hallway, he gave a little shriek. So did Andrew. He hid his face. I patted his shoulder, not taking my eyes off the screen.

"Andrew," I whispered. "You do not have to watch this show. You can go put on your jammies and get ready for bed."

Andrew shook his head, but kept his face hidden.

"It is okay to look now," I told him. "It is not a scary part anymore."

Andrew peeped at the TV. He straightened up and put the pillow down.

"This is a great show," I said. "I love Halloween."

Andrew nodded, his eyes glued to the TV.

"It would be fun to see a real ghost," I said. "A real ghost, or a real goblin, or . . ."

Andrew looked at me as if I were crazy, so I quit talking. But I do think it would be fun

3

to see something real like that. I already know a real witch — old Mrs. Porter, who lives right next door. She does all sorts of witchy things. But I am not supposed to talk about that.

Now Halloween was on its way. I shivered happily. Maybe this year would be the one when I saw a real ghost or goblin!

"Aaah!" cried Andrew again. I winced again. My arm felt like Jell-O. How could he be so scared, when we were sitting in the den in our little house? The little house is cozy and snug and small and safe. It is not like our other house, which is big and noisy and crowded, but also safe.

"Andrew," I whispered. "We are cozy and snug. Everything is fine. We are here in the little house."

Andrew nodded. But he picked up the pillow again.

You know what? I forgot to tell you about our little house and our big house. I will do that right now, while a commercial is on the TV.

4

Cozy Little and Exciting Big

It is true — Andrew and I live at two different houses. Every other month, we live in the little house with our mommy and our stepfather, Seth Engle. During the months in between, we live in the big house with our daddy and our stepmother, Elizabeth. If you are already confused, maybe you had better sit down. It gets a lot more complicated.

You see, a long time ago, Andrew and I lived at the big house all the time, with Mommy and Daddy, when Mommy and Daddy were married to each other. Then

Mommy and Daddy decided that even though they loved me and Andrew very much, they did not want to be married to each other anymore. So they got divorced. Andrew, Mommy, and I moved across town to the little house. Daddy stayed in the big house, because it is where he grew up.

Not long afterward, Mommy met Seth Engle. They fell in love and got married. When they got married, Seth became our stepfather. (Seth is a carpenter. He makes beautiful furniture. He made the desk in my room.) Then Daddy met Elizabeth Thomas, and *they* got married. Elizabeth already had four children, so I suddenly had three new stepbrothers and a new stepsister!

That was when Andrew and I became two-twos. I made up that name for us after my second-grade teacher, Ms. Colman, read us a story called *Jacob Two-Two Meets the Hooded Fang*. Andrew and I are two-twos because we have two mommies, two daddies, two houses, two bikes each, two bedrooms, two sets of clothes and toys, two sets of pets. . . . We have two of almost everything.

This month, October, we were at the little house, with Mommy, Seth, and our little-house pets — Midgie, who is Seth's dog, and Rocky, Seth's cat. The little house is small and cozy and quiet, as I told you before.

Next month, we would be at the big house, with Daddy and Elizabeth. The big house is humongous and noisy and full of people and pets. Besides Daddy, Elizabeth, Andrew, and me, there are five other kids: Sam and Charlie, my stepbrothers who are so old they are in high school already; David Michael, my stepbrother who is seven like me but goes to a different school; Kristy, my stepsister who is thirteen and one of my all-time favorite people; and Emily Michelle, my little sister who Daddy and Elizabeth adopted from a country called Vietnam. Emily is two and a half and very cute.

At the big house we also have Shannon,

who is David Michael's gigundoly big Bernese mountain dog puppy; Pumpkin, who is our fluffy black kitten; my pet rat, Emily Junior (I named her after my little sister); Bob, who is Andrew's hermit crab; and our goldfish, Goldfishie and Crystal Light the Second.

You will not believe this, but one other person also lives at the big house — Elizabeth's mother, Nannie. She is my stepgrandmother. Nannie helps take care of all the people and the pets. I just love her.

Oh! I forgot to mention two other things I have two of. I have two best friends: Hannie Papadakis, who lives across the street and one house down from the big house, and Nancy Dawes, who lives next door to the little house. Hannie and Nancy and I call ourselves the Three Musketeers. The last thing I have two of is glasses: I wear a blue pair for reading things up close, and a pink pair the rest of the time.

There. Now the commercial is over, you

know almost everything about me, and I have to get back to my program.

"What?" Seth shouted suddenly from the kitchen.

Andrew and I stared at each other. What had happened in the kitchen? Had Seth seen a real ghost? Was it something spooky? I grabbed Andrew's hand and pulled him off the sofa.

"Come on!"

A Surprise Adventure

Andrew and I raced into the kitchen.

"What is it?" I yelled. I glanced around the room. Maybe I would see a witch flying back out through the window. Maybe I would see a ghost disappearing into a cupboard. Instead, all I saw was Mommy looking surprised and excited, and Seth talking on the telephone. He wore a big grin on his face, and he made a thumbs-up sign at Mommy.

"What is it, Mommy?" I asked in an indoor voice. (Grown-ups are always telling

me to use my indoor voice.) Andrew and I stood next to Mommy.

Mommy smiled and put her finger to her lips. So Andrew and I had to stand there, burning with curiosity, until Seth got off the phone.

Finally he hung up. He turned to us with a big smile and held out his arms.

"Well, what do you say we all take a little vacation?" he asked.

"Whaaat?" said Andrew and I.

"That was Granny Engle on the phone," explained Seth. (Granny is Seth's mother. She is my stepgrandmother. She lives in Nebraska. Oh — I guess stepgrandmothers are another thing I have two of.)

"How is she?" I asked.

"She is terrific," said Seth. "Especially since she has just won a trip for four to a dude ranch in Colorado!"

My mouth fell open.

"Granny entered a raffle at a fair," Seth continued. "She won the grand prize, which is a trip for four people to a dude ranch for a week. As a special gift, she wants to send the four of us. She will go too and pay her own way. We will be leaving very soon."

"Cool!" I said.

"It does sound like fun," said Mommy.

"What is a dude ranch?" asked Andrew.

"A dude ranch is a place where you can ride horses and live like a real old-time cowboy," explained Mommy.

"Oh, boy!" I shouted. I just love horses. I even have a pony of my own: Blueberry. He lives at a nearby farm. Then I thought of something. "But there are no school vacations coming up," I said. "How can I go?" For a moment I was afraid that my little-house family would go without me.

"I will have to call Ms. Colman," said Mommy. "We will ask for special permission to miss school. You will have to make up all the work you miss," she warned me.

"Oh, boy!" I shouted again. I started to jump up and down. I did not mind the idea

13

of making up all the work. I was too excited about being a real cowgirl!

For the next few days, everything was in a whirlwind as we got ready to go. Ms. Colman gave me permission to miss five days of school. But she gave Mommy a big stack of worksheets for me to fill out. And I had a special assignment: I was supposed to keep a travel journal of my trip and share it with the rest of the class when I returned.

"Okay," I told her. "That sounds like fun!"

"I am glad, Karen," said Ms. Colman. "I hope you have a wonderful time." Ms. Colman is a gigundoly nice teacher.

I have to tell you that the other two Musketeers were not as happy about my trip as I was. I wished I could take them with me, but I could not.

"I will miss you," I told Hannie and Nancy. "I will send you postcards. And show you pictures when I get home."

"We will miss you too," said Hannie.

"But we will try to keep busy while you

are gone," said Nancy. "And when you get back, it will be time for us to make our Halloween costumes!"

"That is right," I said. "By the time I get back, I am sure I will have a terrific idea for my costume." The Three Musketeers hugged.

A Long Way to Colorado

"Up and at 'em, Karen!" Seth said, switching on my overhead light. I sat up in bed and rubbed my eyes. Outside my window, it was still dark. "What time is it?"

"Five-thirty in the morning," Seth said. "We have a plane to catch at seven. So as we cowboys would say — saddle up, partner, it is time to hit the trail."

"Yee-haw!" Andrew hollered. "Giddyap, Thunderbolt!"

I pushed the luggage cart, with Andrew

on top of the pile of suitcases, through the airport terminal. "Ride 'em, cowboy!" I yelled. "Hang on, this bronc is going to buck!"

I slammed on the brakes and jerked the cart from side to side. Andrew whooped and shouted and clutched at the suitcases beneath him.

"Karen! Andrew!" Mommy said sharply. "Do not play roughly in the airport. Andrew, get down from there. Karen, bring the cart over here. It is time to check our bags."

Andrew clambered down, and I pushed the cart to the man in a red jacket and cap. We would be boarding our plane to Colorado in just a few minutes. I was so, so excited!

"May I have more gum, please?" I asked Seth as the plane took off. Seth handed me a stick. I have found that chewing gum on an airplane keeps my ears from getting that yucky underwatery feeling. One stick will do, but three or four is more fun.

I chewed busily and looked around the cabin. ("Cabin" is what the flight attendants call the inside of a plane. This would make more sense if the plane were made of logs.) I adjusted the overhead air-spray-nozzle thingy. I switched my overhead light on and off. I looked out the window. We were in the middle of some clouds, so there was nothing to see. I think clouds are more interesting on the ground, when they are fog.

"I am becoming bored," I announced.

"Read one of your books," said Mommy.

"Okay." I dug out my backpack, which I had stowed ("stowed" is another flight-attendant word) beneath the seat in front of me. I brought out *Danny, the Champion of the World*. That is a book by Roald Dahl. It is about a boy whose father poaches pheasants. It is very good. I have read it four times.

After awhile I put down *Danny*. I was getting bored again. Andrew was asleep. I closed my eyes, but I could not sleep.

I decided to look at all the stuff in the seat-back in front of me. ("Seat-back in front of you" is yet another thing flight attendants like to say.) I read the what-to-do-in-case-of-emergency card. I noted the nearest exit. I opened up the barf bag. I pretended to barf into it until Mommy told me to stop. Too bad Andrew was asleep. I decided to do the pretend-barf thing again as soon as he woke up.

I flipped open the airplane magazine, called *Soar*. It is funny that airplanes have their own magazines. Maybe my school bus should have its own magazine too. I would have to remember to suggest that to the driver when I got home. Most of the airplane magazine was boring. There were articles on places for grown-ups to vacation, how to buy golf clubs, and the different types of caviar. (Caviar is tiny raw fish eggs. People eat them as a treat. Ew.)

Then I came to an article called "John Wayne, King of the Cowboys." Since I was going to be a cowgirl for the next week, I definitely needed to read this article. It turned out to be very interesting. John Wayne was an old-time movie star. He made movies from the 1930s until the 1970s, when he died. He starred in hundreds of Westerns, including all-time classics like *She Wore a Yellow Ribbon*, *Rio Bravo*, and *The Man Who Shot Liberty Valance*. There was a picture of him in the magazine. He was wearing a big white cowboy hat, sitting on a horse in beautiful western country. (I sort of recognized him. I thought maybe I had seen him in some commercials on TV.) He looked exactly like what a cowboy is supposed to look like. I could tell why John Wayne was called King of the Cowboys, and I had never even seen any of his movies. I decided that as soon as we got home, I would ask Mommy to rent *She Wore a Yellow Ribbon*. I liked the title of that one.

I closed the in-flight magazine, and suddenly I felt like closing my eyes. I pictured meeting real cowboys at the dude ranch.

Maybe one of them would look like John Wayne. . . .

I slept until the plane landed and then woke up for the long drive from the airport to the Arrow-A Ranch. That was the name of the ranch where we would be staying. It was three hours away. By the time we arrived at the Arrow-A, the moon was high in the sky and I was ready to go back to sleep.

Seth and Mommy carried Andrew and me to our room in the big ranch house. Mommy tucked me into a twin bed and kissed me good night. Even though I was really excited about being in a new place, I fell asleep right away. A girl can take only so much traveling in one day. Cowgirl adventures would have to wait till morning.

A Big Cowboy Breakfast

I woke up with sunshine staring me in the face. I was starved. I hopped out of bed and looked around. The room I was in was smallish and pretty, with two twin beds. Andrew was in the other bed, still asleep. I saw three doors. Two were open. Through one door I found Mommy and Seth, already dressed. They were waiting for Andrew and me.

After I pulled on a pair of pink jeans and a pink sweatshirt, Granny walked through the other open door. We all had rooms in one big line. There was also a big, old-fashioned bathroom with a gigundo tub that stood on little feet.

I decided that Andrew should get up.

"Come on, Andrew," I said, shaking his shoulder. "Time to go rustle up some grub." Now that I was a cowgirl, I was going to do my best to use Western expressions.

Andrew sat up and said sleepily, "What is for breakfast?"

"Um, I do not know. Maybe in the song 'Home on the Range,' cowboys eat beans and bacon. That might be it."

With Mommy, Seth, and Granny, we left our rooms and headed downstairs. We were staying in a real ranch house. It was very big. Downstairs was one gigundoly huge room. Part of it was a living room and part of it was a dining room and part of it was a kitchen. In the dining room part were two long tables with benches. A big, open kitchen was at one end, with a counter you could see over.

Upstairs was a balcony that went around

the second floor like a U. Ten bedrooms were arranged around the U. At the open mouth of the U was a very wide, polished staircase that led down to the living room area.

When we reached the bottom of the stairs, we followed our noses to the dining area.

"Good morning!" said a friendly-looking woman behind the counter. She had tossed a dish towel over her shoulder. Her blonde hair was pulled into a bun. "I'm Kate — hostess, cook, activities director, and all-around gal Friday."

I liked her right away. Mommy, Seth, Granny, Andrew, and I took our places at one of the long benches.

I was right! There were beans and bacon. There were also eggs (fried, scrambled, poached, or soft-boiled), grits, oatmeal, pancakes with maple syrup or blueberry syrup, applesauce, biscuits, sausage patties, buttered rolls, juice (orange, apple, or tomato), and for the adults coffee or tea.

"Yum!" said Andrew, spreading butter on

a biscuit. I helped myself to a big pile of food and started chewing.

Besides our family, two other families were staying at the ranch. One was a family with two kids — a girl about my age and a boy about Andrew's. Perfect!

I introduced myself to the girl and boy. I am not at all shy about meeting new people. Their names were Jenny and Phil Webb. Jenny wore glasses (like me) and had curly brown hair (not like me). Phil had a big scab on his elbow (Andrew had one on his knee). Jenny and Phil had arrived at the Arrow-A the night before, just like we had. Their parents were Mr. and Mrs. Webb.

The other family staying at the Arrow-A were Mr. and Mrs. Nemchinov and their son, who was also called Mr. Nemchinov. They were all grown-ups.

"Eat up, everybody!" said Kate, setting two more platters piled high with pancakes and sausages on the table. "A big breakfast is a Western tradition. Does anyone know why?"

"Because doing cowboy stuff makes you hungry?" I called out. I love answering questions.

"That is right," said Kate, smiling. "Ranch hands work long hours, and they do not always have time to come back to the house for lunch. So they load up at breakfast. Then they wrap a biscuit or two in a handkerchief, slip that in their saddlebag, and eat lunch on the run — or on the hoof, you might say. And that might be all they have to eat until sundown. So do not be timid around the flapjacks and eggs. By noon, you might wish you had eaten more."

Wow! Eating lunch on horseback! Western life sounded like so much fun, and Kate had (sort of) called all of us at the table "ranch hands." I helped myself to another flapjack and a third slice of bacon.

The younger Mr. Nemchinov asked if the Arrow-A was still a real working ranch.

"Certainly," said Kate. "Cattle have grazed this land for over a hundred and thirty years. And there will be cattle here for another hundred years if my husband and I have anything to say about it."

"How long has the dude ranch been in operation?" asked the older Mr. Nemchinov.

"Why, the Arrow-A has been taking in guests nearly since it was founded," said Kate. "But I will let my husband tell you the story of the ranch. He is the local historian. And here he is now."

Everyone turned to see a tall man in a cowboy hat striding into the dining room.

Kate said, "I would like you to meet the owner of the Arrow-A, Mr. Jonathan Wayne."

Jonathan Wayne tipped his hat. "Howdy, pilgrims," he said in a deep drawl. "You can call me Jon. Jon Wayne."

My mouth dropped open. Jon Wayne! The King of the Cowboys!

Western Riding

"Saddle up, pilgrims," said Jon Wayne a little while later.

All of us guests had gone to the stables, to be fitted out with horses and ponies to ride. Jon had given each of us kids a riding helmet.

He asked us how much experience we had riding horses. The Nemchinovs kept their own horses back in Maryland, where they lived. Since they were good riders, Jon gave them young, fast, energetic mounts.

("Mounts" is cowboy for horses.) Granny, Seth, and Mommy explained that they had not ridden much, so Jon gave them tamer, more sweet-tempered horses.

"How about you, little lady?" asked Jon Wayne.

Now, I knew he was not the real John Wayne. But this Jon Wayne was pretty darn close. He was very tall, he was very wide, and he dressed like a real cowboy: a Western shirt, a big cowboy hat, faded jeans, cowboy boots, and chaps. His face was almost the color of the leather chairs in the ranch living room. I thought he was fabulous.

"I am very experienced," I told him. "I have my own pony, Blueberry, and I went to pony camp."

"Well, then," drawled Jon, "I reckon I will give you Mud Puddle."

My pony, Mud Puddle, was beautiful. He was taller than Blueberry and not as fat. His coat was a lovely, shining brown the color of chocolate. His mane and tail were long and silky. I fell in love with him right away. Andrew got a smaller, shaggy, gray pony named Snickers.

The Webbs had some experience riding too. Jon picked out horses for the grown-up Webbs and ponies for the kids. All of the horses and ponies looked calm and happy and well taken care of.

"This trail we will ride on," said Jon as he swung up into his own saddle, "is wide and easy. It will lead us to a meadow and a stream for the horses to drink from. If anyone gets into a bad patch, give a holler. And you, little fellers," he said to Andrew and Phil, "you stick close by me." He winked at them and they grinned.

Then we moved out. I was sitting in my Western saddle, my feet firmly in the wide stirrups. At pony camp, I had learned how to ride with an English saddle, which is much smaller and lighter than a Western saddle. On an English saddle you can really feel the pony beneath you. On a Western saddle, you feel like you are sitting in a La-Z-Boy recliner. But I got used to it quickly.

"It is pretty here," said Jenny Webb. She was riding behind me. Her mother was behind her.

"Yes, it is," I agreed. "Where are you from?"

"Mississippi," said Jenny. She looked around as our ponies slowly and carefully followed the trail. We were winding down a low hill through some trees, but we could still see some tall, beautiful mountains in the distance. Their tops were purple and orange from the sun. Their lower slopes were covered with a fuzzy blanket of green trees. I heard birds calling above me. The air was fresh and cool on my sweatshirt.

"We only have hills in Mississippi," said Jenny. "No mountains."

"We do not have any mountains in my part of Connecticut either," I said. "Just hills. Big hills."

Up ahead, Jon was pointing out different birds, naming trees, and talking about the local environment.

"Beef cattle are hard on the land," I heard him say. In the distance we could see hills dotted with brown cows. "They chew up the greenery, pack down the earth, and sometimes uproot trees. That's why you need much more land per head of cattle than you do for dairy cows."

Soon we had reached the meadow. We all got off our horses and led them to the stream to drink. The horses seemed to know exactly what to do. They must have been here a lot, I fig — reckoned.

Granny organized my family for some picture taking. Some of us had packed snacks left over from breakfast, and we passed them around. I pulled my travel journal out of my backpack. I uncapped my pen.

I wrote down the names of the birds Jon had pointed out. I wrote down what he had said about beef cattle and dairy cattle. Finally, I wrote this:

IT IS ONLY MY FIRST REAL DAY HERE, AND ALREADY I FELL LIKE A COWGIRL. I HAD BEANS AND BACON FOR BREAKFAST. I AM RIDING IN A WESTERN SADDLE. MAYBE I WILL ASK EVERYONE TO CALL ME COWGIRL KAREN.

Annie Hancock

I groaned softly. "I am stuffed."

I was lying on the Native-American-style rug in front of the huge stone hearth in the living room part of the ranch house. We had finished dinner a little while earlier. I confess: I made a pig of myself.

Lying on the floor next to me, Andrew nodded, his eyes closed. Jenny Webb also moaned softly. Her little brother, Phil, just grunted.

Maybe it was being outdoors all day in the fresh air and sunshine. Maybe it was riding horses, then currying them afterward. (Currying is when you sort of do beauty parlor for your horse.) Whatever the reason, we had all been starving at dinnertime. I had piled my plate with cornbread, beans, roast beef, lima beans, salad, stewed corn, mashed potatoes . . . and fruit cobbler for dessert.

Now I was trying not to think about it.

"Okay, everyone, on your feet!"

I peeped out through half-closed eyes to see Kate Wayne standing above us, a big smile on her face.

"Come on, now, time's a wastin'!" she said, clapping her hands.

"Oh, I'm just a poor, lonesome cowboy," we all sang. It was half an hour later. The ranch guests, plus Jon and Kate and a bunch of their ranch hands, were gathered around a big bonfire outside. We had toasted marshmallows (I managed to eat a few) and watched the sunset. Now we were singing cowboy songs. The air was chilly, but the

fire was warm. The sky was much more black than it ever looks in Connecticut, and the stars were like diamonds. I made a note to write that down in my travel journal.

Kate and Jon and the ranch hands were taking turns teaching us Western songs. I was snuggled between my mommy and Jenny Webb, and I felt so, so happy.

"Tell us about the ranch, Jon," asked Seth a couple of songs later. "How long has it been in your family?"

Jon Wayne stretched his long legs toward the bonfire. "Just about a hundred and twenty years," he said. "My great-grandfather, Jeremiah Wayne, and his family ended up here because of Colorado silver."

"Was there a silver rush here?" I asked.

"A small one," said Jon. "My great-grandfather's family were drawn by the rush. They bought some land, then started to mine for silver. They found some, but not enough to keep the mine open. Eventually most of the silver hunters moved on. But Jeremiah stayed."

"Why?" asked Jenny.

"Because he had met a local girl named Annie Hancock," answered Jon. "My great-grandmother. They fell in love and got married. And Jeremiah decided to stay here and raise beef cattle."

"What a romantic story," said Mommy. "And have there been Waynes here ever since?"

"Yes, ma'am," said Jon. "When Great-grandfather Jeremiah and Annie ran the place, they had the healthiest cattle in the county. Our hands were the best paid and happiest cowboys too. Seems Annie was a genius at the bow and arrow — people came from far and wide to see her shoot, and soon Jeremiah and Annie had the idea of putting those folks up in the ranch house. That's how the dude-ranch operation started up. It was the golden age of the Arrow-A."

The bonfire crackled then. I thought about eating another marshmallow.

"Things looked a little shaky after Jeremiah died," Jon continued. "Annie had to sell off some of the land to keep the ranch going. She did what she had to do, but I believe it took something out of her. The story is, she was never the same after that. Eventually, my grandfather inherited the land. He is the one who told me, when I was a boy, about his parents, Annie and Jeremiah. In time, when my old grandpa died, the Arrow-A belonged to my father. And it became mine last year, when my father passed away."

I looked at our host. I thought Jon Wayne looked sad.

I wondered whether he was sad thinking about Annie having to sell some of the land, and not ever being the same. Or whether he was sad because his grandfather, who told him all those great stories when he was a boy, had died long ago. Or because he was thinking about his own father, who had died the year before. Or because of all those things.

Western Fishing

The next day was a non-horseback riding day. Over breakfast, Kate explained that we greenhorns had to give our legs a chance to recover from the first day of riding. And she was right! My legs were so, so achy from gripping Mud Puddle's back all afternoon.

Mommy and Seth came hobbling down to breakfast looking as if they needed crutches. "We will be okay," Seth assured Andrew and me. "We just need a few minutes, and a couple of cups of coffee, to work out the cricks."

It is amazing how coffee perks up grown-ups. By the time Mommy and Seth stood up from the breakfast table, they were almost able to bend their knees.

That morning, Jon Wayne led us guests across the meadow that spread out behind the house, down to a little river. Piled on the bank were tackle boxes, pairs of tall rubber boots called waders, and fishing poles of several lengths. Jon explained that he would teach fly-fishing to those who wanted to learn. Everyone else could do regular fishing if they wanted, or they could just laze by the bank and watch the river. Granny, Mommy, and Seth wanted to try their hands at fly-fishing. I decided I would watch them for awhile.

Fly-fishing is very, very difficult! It is more than just sticking a worm on a hook (ugh to that, by the way) and dropping the hook in the water. No. With fly-fishing, you use a complicated knot (called a fly, because it looks like a fly) as bait, and you sort of flick your fly and hook over the surface of the water. Using the fly, you try to tease the fish in the water until one of them gets so angry that it leaps up and bites the hook just to show you who is boss. Then you reel it in.

After a few minutes, Jon caught a nice little trout, which he unhooked and threw back in the water. "Catch and release," he called it. "It is better for the river, and for the fish." Then Jon tipped his hat and said, "You will have to excuse me now, folks. I need to go see about a sick calf." He tipped his hat again and walked back toward the house.

I was sorry to see Jon go. He was a lot of fun, and he knew so much about Western things. But he was a cowboy, after all, and not just a dude-ranch host, so he had cowboy jobs to do as well.

I watched Granny, Mommy, and Seth fly-fish for awhile. They were not very good at it. Their lines kept getting tangled up. They did not catch (or release) anything.

I walked downstream a little way, to where Andrew, Jenny, and Phil were skipping stones across a bend in the river. We played in the water together, looking for fish and rocks and interesting hidden things. Jenny found a rock that looked exactly like an arrowhead. We went exploring down the river. We knew we could not get lost, because to find our way home all we had to do was turn around and walk upriver again. After lunch back at the ranch, Jenny taught us to play sardines. It is a kind of hide-and-seek game in which one hider and the seekers all have to crowd into the hiding place once they find the hider. It was fun! Then we went on a nature hike, and identified seven different kinds of trees and collected their leaves. It was another glorious day at the Arrow-A.

Western Archery

On Tuesday morning I bounded out of bed early. "Up and at 'em, pardner," I yelled, whacking Andrew on the shoulder.

"Aughhh!" cried Andrew, sitting up, wide-eyed. "You made me have a nightmare. I thought something had come to get me."

I laughed and threw Andrew his jeans. "Do not be silly, little feller. You did not have time to have a nightmare. Come on! I smell bacon."

Well, let me tell you: The adventure never

stops at the Arrow-A. After we filled up on a big cowboy-style breakfast, Kate told us about the day's activities.

"For grown-ups, there is a challenging trail ride," she told us. "It includes a packed lunch, because you will not be back until the middle of the afternoon. You will see some of the West's most beautiful scenery, though. For the rest of us, a day of fun has been planned. First we will take a short ride to a beautiful nearby rock formation. Then we will have to start getting ready for our big Western hoedown on Saturday night."

A hoedown? That sounded gigundoly fun.

"What is a hoedown?" asked Phil.

"It is like a party and a dance and a barbecue all at once," answered Kate.

"Oh, boy!" I shouted.

Mommy and Seth decided to go on the challenging trail ride. Granny decided to stay with us. I was glad. The younger Mr. Nemchinov went on the trail ride, but his parents stayed. And Mrs. Webb went, while the other Webbs stayed.

After the trail riders left, the rest of us met in the barn and saddled our mounts. Kate and three of the ranch hands led us down a narrow trail. We crossed a shallow stream to a rocky area. Kate pointed out a rock formation that looked like a medieval tower. She said smugglers used to use it as a lookout point. Cool!

Nearby was a small clearing, and we all got off our horses.

"Okay, now," said Kate. "You all know Larry, Punkie, and Bill, right?"

"Right," I called. They were the ranch hands who had come with us.

"Well, Larry is an expert with a rope," said Kate. "Punkie can't be bested with the bow and arrow. And Bill is our resident champion square dancer. They are here to offer lessons to anyone who wants to learn. As for me, I'll be heading back to whip up some lunch in the kitchen. All right?"

"All right!" we cried. Jenny even punched her fist in the air.

"Okeydokey," said Larry with a big smile. "Who wants to learn some ropin'?"

The rest of the day flew by. We all ended up taking turns learning roping, archery, and square dancing. (Archery is when you use a bow and arrow.) At noon we returned to the ranch for a quick lunch and then went right back to our lessons.

Andrew took to the roping right away. Larry showed him how to make a slidey kind of knot. Then he swung the rope in a circle over his head, let it out, and it sailed toward whatever he wanted to rope. Larry said the rope-circle is called a lasso or lariat. Cowboys usually use lassos to capture runaway cows or ponies. Andrew was using his lasso to capture —

"Hey!" I said as the rope settled down over my head.

Andrew giggled and set me free. For the rest of the day, he lassoed everything: fence posts, me, Phil, and even Beany, the

Waynes' basset hound, who simply could not escape fast enough.

"I am the king of the lariat!" crowed Andrew.

As for me, I became queen of the bow and arrow. I do not want to brag, but I have to tell you, I was a natural with the bow and arrow. Punkie lent me a smaller bow than his, and I was using only rubber-tipped safety arrows, but still. I almost always hit what I aimed at.

"I am just like Annie Hancock," I said happily as I knocked over my fifth tin can.

"You do have a natural talent," agreed Punkie.

I think Granny liked the square-dance lessons best. We all had a great time learning how to do-si-do, swing our partners, and turn. By the time Mommy and Seth limped in after their trail ride, the rest of us were ready for the hoedown, only four days away.

"Guess what, Mommy!" I cried. "I know how to shoot a bow and arrow!"

"That's wonderful, honey," said Mommy, sounding tired. She eased herself down into a big, puffy chair and groaned a little bit.

"Did you have a nice ride?" asked Granny.

"Oh, it was lovely," said Mommy. "But I am afraid it was a little too much riding for me. I need to go soak in a hot tub."

"Did you tell everyone what we saw?" asked Seth, sitting gingerly on the edge of the couch.

"Oh, we saw two gray wolves," said Mommy, her eyes lighting up. "They were beautiful, just like silver shadows. And Mrs. Webb thought she may have seen a cougar."

"Cougars are very rare around here," said Jon, taking off his cowboy hat. "But you do see the occasional wolf."

I looked at Andrew. His eyes were wide and blue.

"Wolves?" he whispered. "And a cougar?"

Western Dancing

Sometimes I forget that Andrew is only four going on five. Most of the time he seems almost as old as me. There are times, though, when he seems a lot younger than me. One of those times was right after dinner that evening. We were in our room getting ready for our line-dancing lessons. I had changed into a pair of leggings and a T-shirt. Andrew was sitting on his bed, looking out of the window at the wide, black Colorado sky.

"Karen?" he said. "I think I will stay up

here instead of going to the dance lessons."

"Andrew," I said firmly, "I know what is bothering you. But I promise you that no wolf or cougar will come into the ranch house when it is chockful of people line-dancing to loud music. Now, come on."

Andrew went downstairs with me.

If you have never line-danced before, you do not know that it is gigundoly fun. It is kind of like square dancing, except you all dance in a long line, instead of in a square.

"Mommy, come on!" I called as I sashayed forward and back to the music.

Mommy was perched carefully on the couch. She smiled and waved her hand. I think maybe she was still a little sore from riding. In fact, almost all of the grown-up guests who had gone on the challenging trail ride were either in their rooms or sitting out the line dancing. Since I had been busy all day long, I started to get tired too. I flopped down next to Seth on the couch. He winced.

"Sorry," I said.

"It is okay, honey. It is not your fault I am sore all over."

"Maybe you should take some Motrin," I suggested, just the way Mommy does when I do not feel well. "And a hot bath." It was fun pretending I was the mommy, and Seth and my real mommy were the children. "Then you can go right to bed."

"That sounds good." Mommy moaned. "Is everyone ready to go to bed?"

Andrew and I nodded, and I stood up. All of a sudden, over the loud music, we heard a long, ghostly howl. Then another howl started up, over the first one. Then another. It was a chorus of spooky howls.

Andrew froze, his eyes wide and frightened. I saw him look quickly toward the front door and the back door and the kitchen door. "Wh-what was that?" he whispered, his face white.

Maybe it was Western ghosts! I had been hoping for an extra-spooky Halloween this year. Maybe I would have one.

"I do not know," I said excitedly. "Jon, do ghosts haunt the ranch?"

Jon laughed. He turned off the music, then sat next to Andrew. He patted Andrew on the shoulder, just as the long, low howls started again. All the hairs on the back of my neck stood up. It was great!

"Nope, sorry," said Jon. "I do not want to disappoint you, Karen, but those are ordinary, everyday wolves."

"Wolves?" squeaked Andrew, grabbing Jon's sleeve.

Jon did not seem to mind. "Yessir, wolves. Gray wolves. They howl at night sometimes. They are talking to one another — asking how their day went, I guess."

"You should chase the wolves away from here," said Andrew.

"Oh, no, I would not want to do that. Many people are afraid of wolves, it is true. But wolves are not all bad. In fact, the gray wolf is endangered. People have been working hard to make sure wolves are protected."

"Why?" I asked.

"Years ago," said Jon, "many ranchers tried to get rid of all the wolves in the area. Now, it is true that sometimes wolves will steal a calf or an injured cow. But the ranchers found that without the wolves, the rest of nature got out of balance. For instance, wolves help keep the deer population in check. Without wolves, deer become too numerous. They eat down the vegetation, causing the land to suffer. Without trees and bushes to build their nests in, birds become endangered. Like any other animal, wolves help to keep nature working right." Jon smiled down at Andrew.

"We are lucky to hear those wolves," Jon continued. "Sometimes we do not hear one here at the ranch for weeks on end. That is because wolves are more scared of humans — even small humans — than we are of them. They would rather steer clear of us and the places we live. How about listening again — *shhhh*."

Everyone grew quiet as could be. Andrew had a listening-hard expression on his face.

Outside, the wolves howled again, more faintly this time. They sounded farther away than they had the first time we had heard them. The howls faded, until we could not hear them anymore.

Andrew smiled. "Sounds like they went away."

Jon nodded. "Sounds like it." He gave Andrew's shoulders a squeeze. "Maybe, if you are lucky, they will come back soon, and you will get to hear them one more time before you leave."

"I hope so," said Andrew, yawning. "I cannot wait to tell all my friends at home that I heard real live wolves. Good night, everyone," he said as he went upstairs to our room.

As I followed him, I overheard Mommy say to Jon, "Thank you so much for reassuring Andrew."

I turned around and gazed at Jon. Jon Wayne really was the King of the Cowboys.

Jon Wayne's Problem

On Wednesday morning I was itching to ride Mud Puddle again.

"Oohhhh." Mommy moaned when I asked her to go riding with me. Mommy was eating breakfast standing up at the big kitchen counter. Seth was standing next to her, and so was the younger Mr. Nemchinov and Mrs. Webb. None of them could sit down after their six-hour ride the day before.

"I'd like to go riding too," said Jenny.

"Oohhh." Mrs. Webb moaned.

"I will go with you," said Mr. Webb.

"You can go with me this morning, if you like," said Jon, gulping down some black coffee. "I have to ride fence a little bit. No problem if you want to tag along."

"I do! I do!" I shouted, jumping up and down.

"Me too!" said Jenny. So it was decided.

Granny said she would stay home with Andrew and Phil. Andrew wanted to work on his roping skills. I decided I would practice my archery later in the afternoon. But first I had a date with a horse.

Twenty minutes later I was in my La-Z-Boy Western saddle, sitting high on Mud Puddle's back. Jon was on his big brown-and-white horse. I was behind him, Jenny was behind me, and Mr. Webb was behind her. We were riding slowly on a narrow trail toward what Jon called the east pasture.

"Riding fence means I have to ride alongside some of our fencing and check to see whether it needs repair," explained Jon. "If I see a broken section, I make a note of it. Then my men and I come back to repair it."

"It is a lot of work to keep a ranch running," I said thoughtfully.

"Yes, it is," said Jon. "I never realized how hard my grandfather and father worked to run this place. Until last year, I was only the ranch foreman — not the boss in charge of everything. This past year has been a lot of hard work."

"Tell me more about Annie Hancock," I said as we rode along.

"I never knew her, of course," said Jon. "Most of what I know about her, my grandfather told me when I was little. Annie was his mother, and he adored her. He used to tell wonderful stories about her."

"Like what?" I asked. I was not trying to be nosy. I am just curious. I like to know about everything.

"Well, stories about what a terrific shot she was with her bow and arrow," said Jon. "Stories about how she could hit anything she aimed at — a leaf, a target, a spot on the ground. . . . What I remember best was the way Granddad always seemed to think she could do anything she set her mind to — shooting arrows, herding cattle, running a dude ranch."

We rode along peacefully for a few minutes. It was a beautiful Colorado day. Everything felt so different from Connecticut. The birds were different, the trees were different, my saddle was different. I liked being Cowgirl Karen. I wondered if this was how Annie Hancock had felt.

"Yes, Annie could do anything," Jon said after he had checked a length of fence. "So could Granddad. So could my dad." He straightened up and smiled at me, but it looked as if his eyes did not know his mouth was smiling. "Me, I am not so sure about."

"What do you mean?" asked Jenny. "You are the best!"

"I was a good ranch foreman," said Jon, swinging back up into his saddle. "And sometimes I think I am good at running a dude ranch. But I am not sure I can do both."

He rode on ahead. I let Mud Puddle slow up a bit, until I was riding next to Jenny. I looked at her, and she looked at me.

"Jon seems sad," said Jenny.

"I know," I replied. "He should not be sad. He is a great dude-ranch host! And he seems great at running the ranch."

"He can do both," agreed Jenny.

"But how can we convince him?" I asked. Suddenly, I felt as if we needed to. But I was not sure how. I would have to think about it.

The Granny Chair

DEAR TRAVEL DIARY,

TODAY IS WEDNESDAY. I KNOW I AL-
READY WROTE ABOUT MY MORNING RIDE
WITH JON WAYNE, JENNY, AND MR. WEBB.
BUT NOW I WANT TO WRITE SOME MORE.
YOU ARE GETTING FILLED UP, DIARY! I
CANNOT WAIT TO SHOW YOU TO MS. COLMAN
AND EVERYONE ELSE IN MY CLASS. I AM
HAVING SUCH AN EXCITING AND FUN TIME
THAT I AM SAD IT IS HALF OVER. AT THE SAME
TIME, I MISS HANNIE AND NANCY VERY
MUCH. I WISH THEY WERE HERE TO HAVE
FUN WITH ME. NOT ONLY THAT, BUT HAL-

LOWEEN IS GETTING CLOSER ALL THE TIME.
HALLOWEEN WILL HAPPEN WHEN WE ARE
BACK IN CONNECTICUT, AND I KEEP THINK-
ING ABOUT IT. I DO NOT EVEN HAVE A COS-
TUME YET.

ANYWAY. I WANT TO TELL YOU MORE
ABOUT JON WAYNE, WHO IS THE GREATEST
COWBOY IN THE WORLD. AND I AM NOT
TALKING ABOUT THE MOVIE STAR. I AM TALK-
ING ABOUT OUR HOST. I THINK HE IS GREAT
FOR LOTS OF REASONS: BECAUSE HE IS SO
FRIENDLY, BECAUSE HE LOOKS AND ACTS LIKE
A REAL COWBOY, BECAUSE HE LIKES EVERY-
ONE AND EVERYONE LIKES HIM. BUT I ALSO
THINK HE IS GREAT BECAUSE HE TRULY CARES
ABOUT PEOPLE. HE IS ALWAYS TRYING TO
MAKE PEOPLE HAPPY. LIKE THE OTHER
NIGHT, WHEN HE MADE ANDREW FEEL BET-
TER ABOUT THE WOLVES. (I ALREADY WROTE
IN YOU ABOUT THAT.)

SOMETHING ELSE HAPPENED TODAY THAT
SHOWED ME HOW NICE JON IS. IT WAS THIS
AFTERNOON, AFTER LUNCH. WHEN WE CAME
BACK FROM OUR RIDE, WE FOUND MOST OF

THE GROWN-UPS STANDING AT THE KITCHEN
COUNTER AGAIN. KATE HAD MADE SEVERAL
KINDS OF SALSAS, AND THE GROWN-UPS
WERE HAVING A TASTE TEST. ANDREW TOLD
US THAT HE HAD BEEN PRACTICING HIS ROP-
ING ALL MORNING, AND I BELIEVE IT. HE
ROPED ME TWICE JUST WHILE I WAS TRYING
TO DIP A CHIP!

THEN PHIL WEBB TOLD US ABOUT LOOK-
ING FOR ARROWHEADS BY THE CREEK.
JENNY AND I TOLD EVERYONE ABOUT
OUR RIDE, AND HOW WE HAD SEEN SOME
WILDFLOWERS STILL IN BLOOM, EVEN
THOUGH IT IS OCTOBER.

IT WAS BEAUTIFUL AND WARM IN THE AF-
TERNOON SUN, AND WE KIDS WENT OUTSIDE
TO PLAY FREEZE TAG. ALL THE GROWN-UPS
MOVED OUTSIDE AND WERE TALKING AND
LAUGHING AND TEASING ABOUT STILL
BEING SADDLE SORE FROM RIDING YES-
TERDAY.

THEN I NOTICED MY GRANNY. SHE DOES
NOT EAT SPICY FOOD, SO SHE WAS NOT TRYING
THE SALSA. SHE HAD NOT GONE ON THE LONG

RIDE YESTERDAY, SO SHE WAS NOT BEING TEASED OR LAUGHING. AND SHE WAS NOT A KID, SO SHE WAS NOT PLAYING FREEZE TAG. KATE AND MRS. NEMCHINOV HAD GONE TO THE GROCERY STORE. I REALIZED THERE WAS NO ONE FOR GRANNY TO TALK TO. SHE WAS LEFT OUT.

I WAS JUST ABOUT TO QUIT THE GAME OF FREEZE TAG TO GO TALK TO HER. BUT THEN I SAW JON HEAD TOWARD MY GRANNY.

"MRS. ENGLE!" HE SAID. "SEEING YOU STANDING HERE ON THE PORCH BRINGS BACK WONDERFUL MEMORIES."

"OH?" SAID GRANNY.

"YES. YOU WAIT RIGHT THERE FOR A MINUTE," SAID JON. A FEW MINUTES LATER HE CAME BACK CARRYING A BEAUTIFUL OLD WICKER ROCKING CHAIR. HE SET IT ON THE PORCH AND DUSTED IT WITH HIS RED BAN-DANNA. "THERE YOU GO, MA'AM," HE SAID KINDLY.

"WHY, THANK YOU, JON," SAID GRANNY, SITTING DOWN. "IT IS BEAUTIFUL."

"THAT CHAIR IS CALLED THE GRANNY CHAIR," SAID JON. "IT IS THE VERY CHAIR MY OWN GRANDMOTHER ALWAYS SAT IN. SHE WOULD SIT RIGHT THERE IN THE AFTERNOONS, THE WAY YOU ARE SITTING NOW. FROM THAT CHAIR SHE COULD KEEP AN EYE ON US KIDS WHILE WE PLAYED, LOOK OUT FOR THE MEN COMING HOME FROM THE RANGE, WATCH THE SETTING SUN. I WOULD BE HONORED IF YOU WOULD CONSIDER IT YOUR SPECIAL CHAIR AS LONG AS YOU ARE HERE AT THE ARROW-A."

GRANNY LOOKED HAPPIER THAN SHE HAD LOOKED ALL AFTERNOON. SHE ROCKED BACK AND FORTH SLOWLY, WATCHING US KIDS PLAY FREEZE TAG. SHE WATCHED THE SETTING SUN AND SAW JON'S RANCH HANDS COMING BACK FROM THE RANGE. SHE WAS HAPPY, AND IT WAS ALL THANKS TO JON.

THAT IS WHY I THINK HE IS THE GREAT-EST COWBOY EVER.

The Ghost Town

"I do not want to go to a ghost town," said Andrew firmly on Thursday morning.

"There are no real ghosts, Andrew," said Mommy, taking another bite of flapjack.

"It is just called a ghost town because people used to live there, but no one does anymore," explained Kate as she brought a bowl of fruit salad to the long table. "Nowadays, although no one lives there, it is still a fascinating place. You can visit an old-fashioned general store, a saloon that serves lunches, and a doctor's office preserved as a museum. It is really worth visiting."

"Come on, Andrew," I said. "We will ride there in stagecoaches!"

"All right," said Andrew. "As long as there are no real ghosts."

Twenty minutes later, Jenny and I were waiting for the stagecoach to be brought to the front of the ranch house.

"There it is!" I cried, pointing.

The stagecoach could hold six people inside, plus the driver and another person outside, up high. Jenny, Mommy, Granny, Andrew, Mrs. Webb, and I rode inside. Jon drove, with Mr. Nemchinov (the younger one) sitting beside him. Everyone else rode in an open wagon, on benches. The wagon and the stagecoach were pulled by four horses each.

"Giddyap!" I heard Jon call, and we were off.

Well. If you have never ridden in a stagecoach (and I bet you have not), then you probably do not know that it is not as comfy as it looks. In fact, it is the bounciest, jounciest, teeth-rattlingest ride you can imagine! After just a few minutes I felt as if all my bones were coming unglued. And we were sitting on thickly padded seats! You see, the stagecoach has big wooden wheels, so you feel every single rock, pebble, dip, puddle, and bunch of grass that you roll over!

"How much farther?" asked Andrew. "I am starting to feel carsick. I mean stagecoach-sick."

"Not much farther," Mommy assured him. "I think we are almost there."

The ghost town, which was called Wayne Junction, sat just outside the ranch property. It did not look like a real town — more like a movie set. I saw two rows of old buildings, lining a dusty, dirty unpaved road. The whole thing could not have been more than three blocks long.

"As you see, it is impossible to get lost here," said Jon. "You may look around, have lunch at the saloon, and shop. We can meet back here at one o'clock."

"Ugh." I groaned, rubbing my back. "I think I would rather walk back to the ranch. I do not want to ride in that stagecoach again!"

Mommy laughed and rubbed my back where I could not reach. "Here is the general store," she said. "How about seeing what is inside?"

The general store was not a ghost store. Inside, it was jam-packed with a million and one cool things. It looked just like it did back in the 1870s (a sign said so). I saw wooden barrels of pickles and crackers, sacks of flour and sugar and salt, glass jars of penny candies, and that is not all. There were saddles and bridles and yokes and plows and bolts of cloth. Hams were hanging from the ceiling. I saw tins of coffee and tea. I did not know where to look first.

There were also some new-timey things: postcards, packets of aspirin and Pepto-Bismol, sunscreen. I bought some postcards to send to the other two Musketeers and to my big-house family.

Andrew and I each bought cowboy hats with some money Mommy had given us. Andrew's was red and mine was white. Andrew also bought himself a silver sheriff's badge.

Then we went next door to the barbershop. Everything had been left just the way it used to look, as if the barber would be back any minute. Besides all the hair-cutting things, there were some dentistry tools. Seth read us a sign explaining that in the old West, the barber was often the dentist too. He would cut your hair, then pull your sore teeth — with no pain-killing shot! Yikes, I thought.

Next came the doctor's office museum, which had all sorts of interesting things in it. Medicine back in the old days was pretty gross. You know the expression "bite the bullet"? You say that if something bad happens but you just have to put up with it anyway. In the old days, doctors used to

operate on patients sometimes with no pain-killers, and the patient would be given a bullet to bite on. Well, at the Wayne Junction museum I saw a bullet with tooth marks on it! I am not kidding. That is how hard the patient was biting when the doctor was doing whatever he was doing (and I do not even want to think about what that was).

As much as I love the cowboy days, seeing those tooth marks made me so, so glad I was born in modern times.

I wrote in my journal about the barbershop and the tooth-marked bullet and the saloon (where we had yummy hamburgers and root beer on tap for lunch) and the old broken-down spooky abandoned houses and stables. Wayne Junction was the perfect ghost town.

The Haunted Mine

After lunch, we piled into the stagecoach and wagon again and headed back to the Arrow-A. I rode in the wagon this time, with Seth, Andrew, Jenny, Mommy, and the Nemchinovs. Punkie was our driver. This time Jon took a different route home, the long way around a big flat-topped hill. Jon called the hill a butte. He pronounced the word like this: *byoot*. That is what they call a flat-topped hill in the West.

The road curved around close to the butte. When we were at the base of it,

Jon pulled the stagecoach team to a stop. Punkie stopped the wagon. Everyone hopped down.

"We are back on Arrow-A land now," said Jon. "The ranch house is on the other side of this butte, about a mile and a half away. But right here before us is the most important piece of the Arrow-A's history."

I looked around. I did not see anything except the side of a steep rocky hill and scrubby grass and bushes on the ground.

"Step this way, everyone," said Jon, motioning to us. He disappeared behind a large boulder. We followed him.

On the other side of the boulder, I saw an opening in the hillside — a sort of cave, with big squared-off logs set around the edges. A miniature train track, maybe three feet wide, led into the cave.

"This is the silver mine that Annie Hancock's father, my great-great-grandfather, built," Jon explained. "There was not enough silver to make him a rich man. But there was enough so his family could buy a small piece of land and start their ranch. It is thanks to this hole in the ground that I am a rancher today."

"Can we go in?" I asked. The old mine looked spooky — all dark and lonesome — but really neat.

"Yup," said Jon. "Though of course you cannot go in very far. It was boarded up over eighty years ago, to prevent anyone from going in and getting lost or hurt. Even I have never been past the entrance, though I tried to explore many a time, when I was about your age." Jon winked at me and smiled.

I smiled and winked back. Then cautiously, with the others, I walked into the mine, following the little railroad tracks down a gentle slope into the darkness.

Heavens to Betsy, was it spooky! Black and musty and echoey and damp and chilly. As my eyes adjusted to the dark, I could make out words carved into the timbers holding up the mine. One of them said JONATHAN WAYNE 1965.

"I put that there when I was a little bit older than you," Jon said from behind me.

"Gosh," I said.

About twenty feet in, we came to the end of the shaft. Big rocks, piled up against huge logs jammed in every which way, blocked the tunnel. The light from the entrance behind us was pretty faint. This was the spookiest place of all.

"I bet there are ghosts down here," I said, only half kidding. "The ghosts of miners who were killed in cave-ins."

Jon laughed. "Sorry to disappoint you, but we never had any cave-ins here. No miners were ever killed at the Arrow-A. But the old ranch hands do say there might be a ghost who haunts the mine."

"Really?" I said.

In the weak light I saw Jon nod. "They say my great-grandmother — Annie Hancock Wayne — haunts the mine," he said. "No one knows why she haunts this place. I do not believe it, exactly, myself. But on the other hand, you never know. Maybe Annie is here with us now."

I shivered. A haunted mine! And a mystery — why would Annie haunt it?

15

Western Rain

When we got back to the ranch, it was cool and cloudy. I visited Mud Puddle in the paddock and told him about my morning. He looked very interested. After that, I had a snack of Kate's delicious homemade apple pie, then practiced my archery behind the house. Saturday was the hoedown, and I wanted to be sharp for the show.

Again and again I fitted my rubber-tipped arrow into my Karen-sized bow. Again and again I shot my arrow toward a plastic target tied to a tree. I am not bragging, but most of the time I hit the target. Many times I even hit the bull's-eye! Sometimes I did miss completely, though. Then I just gathered up my arrows and started all over again. I wanted to be as good as Annie Hancock. She was so good that people would come from all over the county just to see her shoot.

While I was practicing, the clouds grew thicker and darker. Soon it was drizzling. Then it started to pour. The ranch hands put all the horses safely in the barn. I put away my bow and arrows. Upstairs in my room, I wrote in my diary.

DEAR TRAVEL DIARY,
   I AM STILL HAVING A FABULOUS TIME HERE AT THE ARROW-A. AFTER THE GHOST TOWN THIS MORNING, WE SAW THE ABANDONED MINE. ANNIE HANCOCK'S GHOST HAUNTS IT! I PRACTICED MY ARCHERY AS SOON AS WE GOT BACK. I THINK I WOULD LIKE A BOW AND ARROWS FOR MY NEXT BIRTHDAY. I AM GET-

THING REALLY GOOD.

NOW IT IS RAINING. IT IS QUIET AND
PEACEFUL. I DO NOT HEAR ANY WOLVES. I
HOPE THEY ARE ALL COZY SNUG IN THEIR
DENS. I AM GOING TO SIGN OFF. I PROMISED
ANDREW I WOULD PLAY CHECKERS WITH
HIM.

TALK TO YOU LATER,
KAREN

Downstairs, I played six games of checkers with Andrew. He won two. I won four.

Then Jenny and I sat on the covered porch, watching the rain fall in great gray sheets across the valley. The sky is so much bigger in Colorado than it is in Connecticut. It was beautiful, watching the rain, but a person can only watch the rain for so long. Soon I turned to Jenny and said, "I am bored."

"Me too," said Jenny.

We went inside to see what the others were doing. Some people were in their rooms, napping. Mommy, Seth, Granny, and

Jon were playing cards. Andrew and Phil were playing checkers.

"Hello, girls," said Kate from behind the kitchen counter. "What are you up to?"

"That is the problem," I said. "We are not up to much. Do you have any ideas about what we could do?"

"Well, let me think," said Kate, tapping her finger against her chin. "We have some old jigsaw puzzles around here."

Jenny and I said (politely) that we were not in the mood for jigsaw puzzles.

"Do you girls like to read?" asked Kate.

"Sure," I said. "I love books. But I have already read the ones I brought, and Jenny's too."

"I have read mine and Karen's also," added Jenny.

"Did you know we have a library in this house?" Kate asked.

"Really?" I said. "A whole library?"

"It is not as big as a regular public library," said Kate. "But guests often bring books and leave them, and we save those books for the new guests. Why, by now we must have hundreds. Including lots that I am sure two seven-year-old girls would be interested in. Let me show you where we keep them."

Kate led us to a room on the second floor, tucked between a linen closet and one of the bedrooms. It was a small room, but it was lined with shelves from floor to ceiling. On the shelves were books and papers and stacks of photographs and magazines and all sorts of stuff.

"The library is kind of messy," Kate said. "But finding something interesting will be fun. You can pretend you are on a treasure hunt."

"We will!" I said as Kate went back downstairs. This was the perfect thing to do on a rainy afternoon.

The Real Annie Hancock

Jenny and I found all kinds of neat things in the Arrow-A library. Life magazines from the 1960s (with pictures of hippies, crew-cut astronauts, and ladies with helmet hairdos). Lots of grown-up books with covers showing bare-chested, long-haired muscle men grabbing women who looked as if they were about to faint. Lots and lots of books by someone named Zane Grey with cowboys on the covers. A stack of ancient (1979 through 1992) *National Geographic* magazines.

There were kids' books too, though most of them were way too old-fashioned. One was called *Talks for Girls*, by the Reverend Aloysius Roche. It was published in 1932. It was all about how girls should be cheerful, polite, clean, and honest. Really! Who would go around thinking you should be grumpy, rude, filthy, and dishonest? Not even Pamela Harding, my best enemy back home, would say that.

Finally Jenny found a stack of Nancy Drews. I had read a couple of Nancy Drews already, and so had Jenny. We took down the stack (there were eight of them) so we could read the titles and try to remember whether we had read them before.

Then I noticed something on the shelf, underneath where the Nancy Drews had been. It was a folder with some old news clippings. One was about Annie Hancock.

"Look!" I said. "Here is a newspaper article about Jon's great-grandmother."

The clipping was from 1972. The article

explained that 1972 was the one-hundredth anniversary of Annie Hancock's birth. It mentioned how famous she had been for her archery. It quoted some old people who still remembered Annie, and what a wonderful host she had been at the Arrow-A Ranch. Last, it mentioned a man named Horace Brigham, a historian who was researching Annie's life for an article for the county historical society.

I looked through the folder. Mr. Brigham's article was not in it. I wanted to find out more about Annie Hancock.

"Time to be Nancy Drew," I said to Jenny.

"Yes," she said. "But how can we get that article? Even if we knew where the county historical society building was, which we do not, we could not get there."

"Maybe not," I said, wiggling my eyebrows. "Then again, maybe we can."

"May we log on to the Internet, please?" I asked Kate a few minutes later. "There is a

Web site I want to show Jenny. A kids' site," I added.

I was being cheerful and polite. And I was pretty clean. But I was not being totally honest. (The Reverend Roche would not approve.) I did want to show Jenny a Web site. But it was not a kids' site. I was hoping the county historical society ran a Web site. I knew Kate and Jon were connected to the Web, because I had seen their computer earlier.

"Sure," said Kate. "I will help you log on."

Kate did, and then she left us alone. I started a search for the county historical society. (Kristy had showed me how to do searches. It is a very handy thing to know.) Bingo! I clicked on the link and called it up. Sure enough, the historical society had put some of its papers on-line, including one by . . . Horace Brigham! And the paper was entitled . . . "Annie Hancock Wayne: Pioneer All Her Life."

After asking permission, Jenny and I printed out a copy of the article and logged off. Then we rushed back to the library with the printout.

Mr. Brigham's article described how Annie had come west with her family from Tennessee when she was nine years old. They had settled on a small plot of land near what is now the Arrow-A Ranch when, one day, little Annie was playing in a cave and picked up a solid silver nugget the size of her thumb.

That nugget set off a silver rush that brought prospectors from all over the world to this part of Colorado. With the money from the nugget, Annie's family was able to buy most of the land that now made up the Arrow-A Ranch. As a special present, Annie's parents bought her a fancy bow-and-arrow set, which Annie had always wanted. Just as Jon had told us, they named the ranch — the Arrow-A, for Arrow Annie — after her.

Soon after, Annie met Jeremiah Wayne, whose family had come to Colorado in the silver rush. The Waynes had not found much silver, but they had staked out a small ranch next door to the Arrow-A. When they grew up, Annie and Jeremiah married. The two ranches merged, to become the largest ranch in that part of Colorado. It was only years later, when Annie was an old woman, that she was forced to sell off the part of the ranch that had originally been the Waynes' property, returning the Arrow-A to its original size.

"Wow!" I said when we finished reading. "That is a great story! Annie herself was the one who started the silver rush — "

"The same silver rush that brought her future husband's family to Colorado!" finished Jenny.

"Hey!" I said. "Maybe *that* is why she haunts the mine. It is the place where she found the silver nugget and changed her whole life. If she had not found that nugget, she never would have gotten her fancy bow-and-arrow set and become a famous archer."

"Her family would never have owned the Arrow-A," said Jenny.

"She never would have met her husband," I added. "I am sure that is it. Annie's ghost is not sad. She haunts the mine because that is where all her happiness began!"

The Real Jon Wayne

DEAR TRAVEL DIARY,

NOW JENNY AND I KNOW WHAT WE HAVE TO DO. WE ARE GOING TO SPEND ALL DAY DOING IT. I CAN'T STOP TO TELL YOU ABOUT IT NOW. I ALREADY HEAR JENNY CALLING ME. TOMMORROW, SATURDAY, IS THE BIG HOEDOWN, AND OUR LAST DAY HERE AT THE ARROW-A. IF OUR PLAN WORKS, I WILL TELL YOU ABOUT IT. IF OUR PLAN DOES NOT WORK... WELL, THEN I DO NOT KNOW IF THE ARROW-A WILL STILL BE HERE NEXT YEAR. MORE LATER!

   LOVE,

   KAREN

After breakfast on Friday, Jenny and I met in the library on the second floor. Everyone had already decided what they were going to do that day: Mommy, Seth, and Granny were visiting a nearby artists' colony, to see some potters and some silversmiths. Seth is an artist with wood, and Mommy makes artistic jewelry, so they were very interested in seeing other people's work. The Webbs had taken Andrew with them on a short trail ride. (Mrs. Webb groaned when she got back on her horse, but she did it.) The Nemchinovs headed back to Wayne Junction to do more shopping. Kate had said it was fine if Jenny and I stayed with her. She said she would even go riding with us later.

"Ready?" I asked Jenny now in a whisper.

"Ready!" she answered, and we headed into the library. We were about to put our secret plan into action — our plan to help Jon Wayne decide to remain the host of the Arrow-A. Every time he had talked about the ranch during the past week, he had seemed sad, as if he did not know what to do. He was not sure he was living up to his father's past, and his grandfather's. He did not seem sure that he should keep the Arrow-A going. Jenny and I had a plan that we hoped would show Jon that he was doing a great job.

The day before, when we were being Nancy Drew, we had noticed a stack of guest books on one shelf. They were books that went back almost twenty years. In them, guests had written about their visits to the Arrow-A.

Now Jenny and I read through them, looking for certain things. When we found a certain something, we carefully copied it down in a notebook.

That took us almost all morning. Then, at lunchtime, one by one, we talked to the other guests at the Arrow-A. We asked them questions and wrote down their answers.

Later still, Jenny and I went to the stable and asked Punkie and Bill if they would take us riding. While we were riding, Jenny and I interviewed the hands about Jon

Wayne. We asked them questions and wrote down their answers. After we got back, we talked to Larry for a long time.

That evening, Jenny and I holed up in the library until bedtime. Kate had given us some construction paper, scissors, and glue. She had also given us permission to cut pictures out of some old magazines. We worked and worked like worker bees until Mommy and Mrs. Webb told us to get ready for bed. By then, we were just about finished with our secret project. It had taken almost all day, but it had turned out great. Jenny and I made secret signs at each other as our mommies led us away. We would put our plan into action the next day — at the hoedown.

The Wild, Wild West

Saturday was our very last full day at the Arrow-A. On Sunday morning we would all board planes again, to take us back to the places we had come from. I knew that no matter what happened, I would never forget my week at the dude ranch — a whole week of being Cowgirl Karen.

Luckily, Saturday was beautiful and clear. It was a little cooler, as if autumn was finally deciding to settle down here at the Arrow-A. In the morning, my family and I took a nice long ride, saying good-bye to all our favorite places, taking last-minute pictures. I had brought Mud Puddle a whole apple for himself, for being such a good pony.

Then, after lunch, the party began. First, the ranch hands demonstrated their special tricks, while we guests sat on fence rails and whooped and hollered. Punkie, Larry, and Bill showed us some fancy rope tricks, spinning their ropes and jumping in and out of them and lassoing fence posts over their shoulders. Punkie even threw a tin can in the air and lassoed it before it hit the ground.

"I am going to have to practice even more," said Andrew, looking determined. I sighed. I knew that he would be practicing on me as soon as we got home.

Then four of the ranch hands sang a bunch of songs in a barbershop quartet. That is when four people sing with no music, and make their voices blend and mix in a really neat way. They wore red-striped shirts and bow ties. They were awesome!

Then it was the guests' turn. We showed what we had learned during the week —

whether it was a song, some dancing, some roping, some fly-fishing styles, or . . . shooting arrows.

I have to tell you, I won the prize for most accurate shot. I was so proud! Seth took a picture of me holding up my certificate, which Jon and Kate had filled out.

After everyone had demonstrated a talent, it was time for the barbecue. The smell of barbecue cooking outside had been driving me crazy all afternoon. Now I piled my plate high, and sat on the porch steps to eat.

I was hardly finished with my plate of seconds when Kate called out, "Swing your partner, folks!"

For the square dance, the furniture had been cleared out of the living room/dining room area on the first floor. A five-piece band was set up at one end, with a guitar, harmonica player, bass fiddle, violin, and accordion. The musicians started playing, and the music was so fun and dancey that I felt as if everyone in the world would have to get up and dance to it.

We wove in and out of our square, going forward and back and around and twirling and dipping and swinging until I could hardly breathe. Granny's face was flushed, and Mommy was laughing as Seth spun her around. Everyone was smiling and joking and the room was filled with happiness and shining faces. My heart felt as if it would burst.

Then I saw Jenny motion to me.

I sidled over to her.

"Now?" she whispered loudly over the music.

"Now!" I said. And we set our plan in action.

Annie and Jon — Happy at Last

During a break in the music, Jenny and I dashed to my room, where we had stored Jon's surprise. Then we ran back to the hoedown and found Jon. He was standing by a punch bowl, ladling "Western Brew" (actually it was cranberry juice and club soda) into a cup.

"Howdy, pilgrims," Jon greeted us.

"Jon, we must talk to you," I said in an important voice.

"It is critical that we speak," added Jenny.

Jon raised his eyebrows. "All right. I can

see that you are serious. We should find a quiet place."

The three of us went into the study off the main room and shut the door. We sat down.

"Now, what did you want to discuss?" Jon asked. "You have been having a good time at the Arrow-A, right?" He looked concerned.

"Of course we have!" I said. "We love the Arrow-A. It is the best dude ranch ever. We are not here to complain — just the opposite."

"We know that you are not sure you want to keep running the Arrow-A," Jenny said. "And we think you definitely should."

I handed Jon the folder of guest-book quotations and interviews with current guests and ranch hands. In our best handwriting, we had copied exactly what some guests had said. Things like, "Thanks to Jon, our stay here was terrific!" Or, "Thank you, Jon, for teaching me how to tie a fly." And, "I was always scared of horses until I came here. Thank you, Jon."

The ranch hands had nice things to say too. "Jon was a fine foreman, but he is even better being the big boss," said Bill. "Jon handles both jobs well," said Punkie. "If Jon wants to focus on being the dude-ranch host, I will be happy to be ranch foreman," said Larry. Jenny and I had decorated the folder with cutout pictures of cowboys, cows, flowers, and a sunset. I was tingling with excitement.

"What do we have here?" said Jon, opening the folder.

Jon slowly read through all the pages of the folder. I saw him turn to the last page. There, I had written:

JON, YOU ARE THE BEST COWBOY EVER. ALL THE RANCH HANDS SAY SO. BUT MORE THAN THAT—YOU ARE ALSO THE BEST DUDE-RANCH HOST EVER. YOU HELPED ANDREW WHEN HE WAS SCARED OF WOLVES. YOU MADE MY GRANNY FEEL AT HOME. AND LOOK AT ALL THE QUESTS, ALL THROUGH THE YEARS, WHO SAY THAT YOU MADE THE ARROW-A SPECIAL. THANK YOU, FROM ALL OF US.

Then Jenny and I had signed our names.

Jon cleared his throat, then slowly closed the folder. "You girls are mighty sweet to have made this for me," he said. "And I appreciate what you are trying to do. But the Arrow-A has had its share of sadness over the years. Now, I do not exactly believe that Annie Hancock's ghost haunts that old silver mine. But I do not exactly *not* believe it either. I have to wonder if the Waynes would not be better off giving up the land and moving on. . . ." His voice trailed off.

"Jon, you are going to be surprised by what I have to show you," I said, smiling. I handed him the printout of the article by Horace Brigham. "If Annie haunts the mine, it is not because she was sad there. It is because that is where she was happiest."

Jenny and I waited quietly for a few minutes while Jon read Horace Brigham's article. "Why, for goodness' sake!" he murmured.

Finally he put the printout down. "I never knew that Annie's archery career got started when she found the silver nugget. And I never knew that the land she sold off, when she was an old lady, had not been part of the original Arrow-A. Somehow that makes it less sad. I think you girls are right. If Annie does haunt the mine, it is because it is the place that made her life the wonderful adventure it turned out to be."

Jenny and I smiled at each other.

Jon said, "Knowing that Annie's happy memories keep her at the ranch will make me think twice — even three times — about leaving it."

"Hooray!" Jenny and I shouted. We traded high fives, then gave Jon a huge hug.

Back East Again

The airplane ride home was so, so sad. We were hardly in the air, and I missed the Arrow-A already.

I did not feel like listening to country music on my little airplane headphones. I did not feel like looking at the pictures Mommy and Seth had taken at the ranch. I did not feel like reading. I did not even feel like pretending to heave into the barf bag.

Andrew looked sad too. He had wanted to hear wolves howling one more time, but they had not returned to the ranch.

"I miss Jon Wayne," Andrew said.

"Me too," I replied. I started to tear up a little. "I wish I could live forever at the Arrow-A."

Mommy patted my leg. "That sure was a fun week. Did you think so too?"

I nodded.

"There will be so much to tell Hannie and Nancy when we get home," said Mommy.

"Yes," I said, brightening. "I cannot wait to tell them all about Jon Wayne, the king of the cowboys. And Annie Hancock, who was a pioneer all her life. And about riding the range, and shooting arrows, and square-dancing at the hoedown, and — "

Mommy laughed. "You certainly do have a lot to tell."

"And the haunted mine!" I finished. "That was the best thing of all, I think. It was so spooky! And hey, that reminds me — Halloween is coming up. And I know just what I am going to dress up as."

"What will you be, Karen?" Mommy asked.

111

"I will dress up as Annie Hancock. Not the mine-haunting, ghostly Annie, but the arrow-shooting, ranch-running Annie. No one in Stoneybrook will know who she was, but that is okay. I will look like a cowgirl, and that is a good costume. But I will know that I am not just any cowgirl. I will be Annie Hancock, Queen of the Cowgirls."

"That is a wonderful idea, Karen," said Mommy. "And Andrew, do you know what you will dress up as?"

"A wolf!" he replied. "Listen to my howl: Ooh-ooh-arrooooooo!"

Just then a flight attendant passed by. "Goodness!" she said. "I believe there is a wolf on this plane."

Andrew laughed. "No, it was only me! Do not be scared. Wolves are endangered, you know. And they are related to dogs."

I smiled. I felt better. We were flying back to our home and friends in Connecticut. I had a whole stack of finished worksheets to give to Ms. Colman, as well as my almost-filled-up travel diary. Hannie and Nancy were waiting for me. I hoped that someday I would return to the Arrow-A. But I knew that even if I never got to Colorado again I would always remember the Arrow-A: the things I learned, the friends I made, the land I saw.

I joined Andrew in a loud wolf howl.

And nobody even told us to use our indoor voices.

About the Author

ANN M. MARTIN lives in New York City and loves animals, especially cats. She has two cats of her own, Gussie and Woody.

Other books by Ann M. Martin that you might enjoy are *Stage Fright*; *Me and Katie (the Pest)*; and the books in *The Baby-sitters Club* series.

Ann likes ice cream and *I Love Lucy*. And she has her own little sister, whose name is Jane.

BABY-SITTERS™
Little Sister
by Ann M. Martin
author of The Baby-sitters Club®

More Titles... ➡

❑	MQ69188-0	#80	Karen's Christmas Tree	$2.99
❑	MQ69189-9	#81	Karen's Accident	$2.99
❑	MQ69190-2	#82	Karen's Secret Valentine	$3.50
❑	MQ69191-0	#83	Karen's Bunny	$3.50
❑	MQ69192-9	#84	Karen's Big Job	$3.50
❑	MQ69193-7	#85	Karen's Treasure	$3.50
❑	MQ69194-5	#86	Karen's Telephone Trouble	$3.50
❑	MQ06585-8	#87	Karen's Pony Camp	$3.50
❑	MQ06586-6	#88	Karen's Puppet Show	$3.50
❑	MQ06587-4	#89	Karen's Unicorn	$3.50
❑	MQ06588-2	#90	Karen's Haunted House	$3.50
❑	MQ06589-0	#91	Karen's Pilgrim	$3.50
❑	MQ06590-4	#92	Karen's Sleigh Ride	$3.50
❑	MQ06591-2	#93	Karen's Cooking Contest	$3.50
❑	MQ06592-0	#94	Karen's Snow Princess	$3.50
❑	MQ06593-9	#95	Karen's Promise	$3.50
❑	MQ06594-7	#96	Karen's Big Move	$3.50
❑	MQ06595-5	#97	Karen's Paper Route	$3.50
❑	MQ06596-3	#98	Karen's Fishing Trip	$3.50
❑	MQ49760-X	#99	Karen's Big City Mystery	$3.50
❑	MQ50051-1	#100	Karen's Book	$3.50
❑	MQ50053-8	#101	Karen's Chain Letter	$3.50
❑	MQ50054-6	#102	Karen's Black Cat	$3.50
❑	MQ50055-4	#103	Karen's Movie Star	$3.99
❑	MQ50056-2	#104	Karen's Christmas Carol	$3.99
❑	MQ50057-0	#105	Karen's Nanny	$3.99
❑	MQ50058-9	#106	Karen's President	$3.99
❑	MQ50059-7	#107	Karen's Copycat	$3.99
❑	MQ43647-3		Karen's Wish Super Special #1	$3.25
❑	MQ44834-X		Karen's Plane Trip Super Special #2	$3.25
❑	MQ44827-7		Karen's Mystery Super Special #3	$3.25
❑	MQ45644-X		Karen, Hannie, and Nancy The Three Musketeers Super Special #4	$2.95
❑	MQ45649-0		Karen's Baby Super Special #5	$3.50
❑	MQ46911-8		Karen's Campout Super Special #6	$3.25
❑	MQ55407-7		BSLS Jump Rope Pack	$5.99
❑	MQ73914-X		BSLS Playground Games Pack	$5.99
❑	MQ89735-7		BSLS Photo Scrapbook Book and Camera Pack	$9.99
❑	MQ47677-7		BSLS School Scrapbook	$2.95
❑	MQ13801-4		Baby-sitters Little Sister Laugh Pack	$6.99
❑	MQ26497-2		Karen's Summer Fill-In Book	$2.95

Available wherever you buy books, or use this order form.

Scholastic Inc., P.O. Box 7502, Jefferson City, MO 65102

Please send me the books I have checked above. I am enclosing $_____ (please add $2.00 to cover shipping and handling). Send check or money order – no cash or C.O.Ds please.

Name_____Birthdate_____

Address_____

City_____State/Zip_____

Please allow four to six weeks for delivery. Offer good in U.S.A. only. Sorry, mail orders are not available to residents of Canada. Prices subject to change.

BSLS998

PIXIE TRICKS

Seeing Is Believing

☐ BFB 0-439-17218-7	**#1: Sprite's Secret**	$3.99 U.S.
☐ BFB 0-439-17219-5	**#2: The Greedy Gremlin**	$3.99 U.S.
☐ BFB 0-439-17978-5	**#3: The Pet Store Sprite**	$3.99 U.S.

Available wherever you buy books, or use this order form.

visit us at www.scholastic.com